I WILL NEVER GET A STAR ON MRS. BENSON'S BLACKBOARD

Jennifer K. Mann

CANDLEWICK PRESS

I WILL NEVER get a star on Mrs. Benson's blackboard.
Mrs. Benson gives stars for stuff like spelling or neatness
or raising your hand and saying the right answer.

Not for doodling or daydreaming.

One morning when we were doing pluses and minuses, I raised my hand to give the answer. But when I went up and put it on the board, Mrs. Benson said,

"Rose . . ."

I definitely didn't get a star for math.

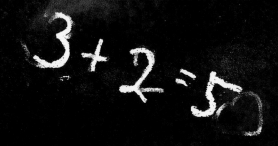

I really wanted to get a star, so later I raised
my hand to read out loud. But Mrs. Benson
stopped me after only one line and said,

"Rose . . ."

I tried to be louder, but I know I definitely
will never get a star for reading.

That afternoon, a man named Mr. Sullivan came
to visit our class. He told us about being an artist,
and we looked at his paintings.

I was still thinking about it
while I served the snack . . .

Whoops!

I knew Mrs. Benson definitely would never ever
put a star next to my name now.

At the end of the day, Mrs. Benson said that
she was going to check our desks for neatness.

I wondered if Mrs. Benson was the kind of teacher who dumps messy desks on the floor. I got butterflies in my stomach.

She pulled out Alan's bologna sandwich.

She refused to touch Jodi's wad of tissues.

But Sam's desk was spick-and-span.

A star for you, Sam!

I was the last kid in the last row.
I knew my mess was worse than an old sandwich or tissues.

And now I had a big tummy ache.

Then, just as Mrs. Benson finished looking at the
desk in front of mine, the bell rang.

As the rest of the kids grabbed their bags, Mrs. Benson
said, "Close call, huh, Rosey? I'll look at yours tomorrow."

I got to school early the next morning so
I could make my desk spick-and-span.

That afternoon, Mrs. Benson said we could make
thank-you cards for Mr. Sullivan.

I got out all my art supplies and made a super-gigantic
card with paintings on both sides.

Then I saw Mrs. Benson coming to check my desk—
and now it was messier than ever!

I felt sick.

Then she said,

"Rose . . ."

I looked up.

Mrs. Benson was laughing!

Then I looked down.

My desk was covered in paint.
And so was I.

Then everyone else started laughing.

And I did, too.

Then Mrs. Benson looked at my card and said,
"Rose! You are a true artist, just like Mr. Sullivan.
Class, we can put all the other cards
in Rose's big card while she cleans up."

It wasn't easy,

but I scrubbed my desk
and cleaned up all
my art supplies,

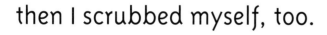

then I scrubbed myself, too.

And finally, my desk and I were clean again.

Right before the bell, Mrs. Benson drew
all the stars for the day. When she was
finished, she called me up to the board.

"Rose . . ."

Uh-oh.

I walked up to the front of the room.
Then Mrs. Benson handed me
the chalk and told me
to draw a star by my name.

Finally!

I got a star on
Mrs. Benson's blackboard—

and so did she!

To Holly, for believing utterly in this book from the very start,
and to Kate and Heather, for making it come true

AUG 2 8 2015.

First edition 2015

Library of Congress Catalog Card Number 2013957526
ISBN 978-0-7636-6514-2

15 16 17 18 19 20 CCP 10 9 8 7 6 5 4 3 2 1

Printed in Shenzhen, Guangdong, China

This book was typeset in Triplex.
The illustrations were done in a mix of ink, gouache, and digital collage.

Candlewick Press
99 Dover Street
Somerville, Massachusetts 02144

visit us at www.candlewick.com